James C. Edwa

The Little Red Lounge. Or, Beechers Fix January and May in a New Dress

James C. Edwards

The Little Red Lounge. Or, Beechers Fix January and May in a New Dress

Reprint of the original, first published in 1875.

1st Edition 2024 | ISBN: 978-3-38538-812-3

Verlag (Publisher): Outlook Verlag GmbH, Zeilweg 44, 60439 Frankfurt, Deutschland
Vertretungsberechtigt (Authorized to represent): E. Roepke, Zeilweg 44, 60439 Frankfurt, Deutschland
Druck (Print): Books on Demand GmbH, In de Tarpen 42, 22848 Norderstedt, Deutschland

THE

Little Red Lounge;

OR,

BEECHER'S FIX

JANUARY AND MAY IN A NEW DRESS.

BY GINGER.

NEW YORK:

1875.

THE LITTLE RED LOUNGE;

OR,

BEECHER'S FIX.

THERE lived in Brooklyn, high above the bay,
A Pastor old, with spirit light and gay;
Of gentle manners as of generous race,
Blest with much sense, true inwardness and grace.
Yet, led astray by VENUS' soft delights,
He scarce could rule some idle appetites ;
For all we know, since NOAH and the flood,
The best of pastors are but flesh and blood.

Now, in due time, when sixty years were o'er,
Old BEECHER saught a friendly neighbor's door.
Whether true holiness inspired his mind,
Or kissing turned his brain, is hard to find;
But his high courage pricked him forth to love,
And to inspire his neighbor's gentle dove.
This was his nightly dream, his daily care,
And to ELIZABETH his constant prayer,

Once, ere he died, to taste the blissful life,
And full enjoyment of a neighbor's wife.
Deeply he loved, with carnal passion high,
And sighed for love, with all it could imply.
Loose creeds he fortified in Plymouth fane,
And daily gained new converts to his train.
Grave authors say and witty poets sing,
That honest wedlock is a glorious thing;
Which we confess; yet, there is, to boot,
A great enjoyment oft in stolen fruit.
Our Pastor chose a damsel young and fair,
To bless his age and wanton with his hair ;
His lips to kiss, and, free from noise and strife,
Conduct him gently through the cares of life.
Some married men may bear their yoke with ease,
Secure at once themselves and Heaven to please ;
And pass their inoffensive hours away,
In bliss all night, and innocence all day ;
Though fortune change, their constant wives remain,
Augment their joys, or mitigate their pain.

But what so pure that envious tongues will spare ?
Some wicked wits have libeled all the fair ;
With matchless impudence they style a wife
The dearbought curse, and lawful plague of life ;
A bosom serpent, a domestic evil,
A night invasion and a mid-day devil.
Let not the wise these slandrous words regard,
But curse the bones of every lying bard ;

All other goods by fortune's hands are given,
A wife is the peculiar gift of Heaven.
Vain fortune's favors, never at a stay,
Like empty shadows, pass and glide away ;
One solid comfort, our eternal wife,
Abundantly supplies us all our life ;
This blessing lasts with some, it is most true,
As long as heart can wish, and longer too.

Our grandsire ADAM, ere of EVE possess'd,
Alone and even in Paradise unbless'd,
With mournful looks the blissful scenes survey'd,
And wander'd in the solitary shade;
The Maker saw, took pity and bestow'd,
Woman the last, the best reserved of God.
A wife ! ah, gentle deities can he
That has a wife e'er feel adversity ?
Would men but follow what the sex advise,
All things would prosper, all the world grow wise.
'Twas by REBECCA's aid that JACOB won
His father's blessing from an elder son ;
Abusive NABAL owed his forfeit life
To the wise conduct of a prudent wife;
Heroic JUDITH, as old Hebrews show,
Preserved the Jews, and slew the Assyrian foe; At
HESTER's suit, the persecuting sword
Was sheathed, and ISRAEL lived to bless the Lord.

These were great motives with the Pastor
sage, And in secret letters he did engage.

A wife's a wife so long as love is bliss,
But wintry age will chill the sweetest kiss.
When wives grow old their merry fits are o'er,
And love without those fits is sure a bore.
His friends were summoned on a point so nice,
To pass their judgment, and to give advice; But
fix'd before, and well resolved was he,
(As men that ask advice are wont to be.)

My friends, he cried (and cast a mournful
look Around the room, and sigh'd before he
spoke), Beneath the weight of three score years
I bend, And, worn with cares, and hastening to
my end; How have I lived indeed you know too
well,
In God's good ways, I'm not asham'd to tell.
But gracious Heaven has ope'd my eyes at last;
With due regret I view some vices past,
And, as the precept of my Church decrees,
The gentler sex I must engage to please.
But since by counsel all things should be done,
And many heads are wiser still than one, Choose
you for me, who best shall be content
When my desire's approved by your consent.

One caution yet is needful to be told,
To guide your choice, the dame must not be old.
There goes a saying, and 'twas shrewdly said,
Old fish at table, but young flesh in bed.
My soul abhors the tasteless, dry embrace
Of a stale virgin with a wintry face;

Give me the girl who knows the work on hand, And
fills, without being taught, the soul's demand. No
crafty widows shall approach my bed,
Upon their breasts I dare not trust my head.
As subtle clerks by many schools are made,
Those widow'd dames are mistresses o' th' trade;
But young and tender wives, ruled with ease,

We form like wax, and mold them as we please.

Conceive me, Sirs, nor take my sense amiss,
'Tis what concerns my life's eternal bliss;
For, since I find no pleasure in my wife,
With all my honors, I abhor this life.
She that is blest with store of grace divine,
May live a saint by love's consent and mine.
And, since I speak of passion, let me say
(As, thanks my stars, in modest truth I may),
My limbs are active, still I'm sound at heart,
And a new vigor springs in every part.
Think not my pith is lost, tho' time has shed
These reverend honors on my hoary head;
Thus trees are crown'd with blossoms white as snow,
The vital sap then rising from below;
Old as I am, my lusty limbs appear,
Like winter greens, that flourish all the year.
Now, Sirs, you know to what I stand inclin'd,
Let every friend with freedom speak his mind.

He said ; the rest in different parts divide; The
knotty point was urged on either side;

Love was the theme on which they all declaim'd:
Some praised with wit, and some with reason blam'd;
Till, what with proofs, objections and replies,
Each wondrous positive, and wondrous wise,
There fell between his brothers a debate,
Woodhullism this was called, and Free-Love that.

First to the Pastor, MOULTON thus begun,
(Mild were his looks, and pleasing was his tone):
Such prudence, Sir, in all your words appears,
As plainly proves, experience dwells with years.
Yet you pursue sage SOLOMON'S advice,

To work by counsel when affairs are nice;
But, with the wise man's leave, I must protest,
So may my soul arrive at ease and rest,
As still I hold my own advice the best.

Sir, I have lived a Christian all my days,
And dearly loved your bold old Plymouth ways;
I have observed this useful maxim still,
To let my betters always have their will;
Nay, if my Priest affirmed that black was white,
My word was this, " Your holy mind is right. "
The assuming wit, who deems himself so wise
As his mistaken patron to advise,
Let him not dare to vent his dang'rous thought;
A noble soul was never in a fault.
This, Sir, affects not you, whose every nod
Is weigh'd with judgment, and befits a god.

Your will is mine; and is (I will maintain)
Pleasing to God, and should be so to man;
At least your courage all the world must praise,
Who dare to nest-hide in these sober days.
Indulge the vigor of your mounting blood,
And let gray fools be indolently good,
Who, past all pleasure, damn the joys of sense,
With reverend dullness and grave impotence.

CADY, who silent sat, and heard the man,
Thus, with a philosophic frown, began:

A heathen author of the first degree,
(Who, tho' not faith, had sense as well as we,)
Bids us be certain our concerns to trust
To those of generous principles, and just.
The venture's greater, I'll presume to say,
To give your person, than your goods away;
And, therefore, Sir, as you regard your rest,
First learn the lady's qualities at least;
Whether she's chaste or rampant, proud or civil;
Meek as a saint, or haughty as the devil;
Whether an easy, fond, familiar fool,
Or such a jade as no man e'er can rule.
'Tis true, perfection none must hope to find
In all this world, much less in womankind;
But if her virtues prove the larger share,
Bless the kind fates, and think your fortune rare.
Ah, gentle Sir, take warning of my friend,
Who knows too well the state you thus commend,

And, spite of all his wisdom, must declare,
All he can find is bondage, cost, and care.
Heaven knows, he sheds full many a private tear,
And sighs, in silence, lest the world should hear;
While all his friends applaud his blissful life,
And swear that he must have a charming wife,
Demure and chaste as any vestal nun,
The meekest creature that beholds the sun!
But, by the immortal powers, he feels the pain,
And he that smarts has reason to complain.
Do what you lists, for me; you must be sage,
And cautious sure; for wisdom is in age;
But at your years, to venture on the fair !
By Him who made the ocean, earth and air,
To please a wench, when her occasions call,
Would busy the most vigorous of you all.
And, trust me, Sir, the chastest you can choose
Will ask observance, and exact her dues.
If what I speak, dear BEECHER, doth offend,
Remember, Sir, Dame STANTON is your friend.

'Tis well, 'tis wondrous well, Old WARD replies;
Most worthy woman, faith you're mighty wise !
We, Sirs, are fools, and must resign the cause
To heathenish authors, proverbs and old saws.
He spoke with scorn, and turn'd another way:—
What does my friend, my own dear BOWEN say?

I say, quoth he, by heaven we're much to blame,
To pick at flaws that should be woman's fame.

At this the council rose, without delay:
Each, in his own opinion, went his way;
With full consent that, all disputes appeased,
BEECHER should fondle whom and what he pleased.

Whose now but BEECHER's heart exults with joy?
The charms of woman all his soul employ:
Each nymph by turns his wavering mind possest,
And reigned the short-lived tyrant of his breast.
Whilst fancy pictured every lively part,
And each bright image wander'd o'er his heart.
Thus, in some public forum fix'd on high,
A mirror shows the figures moving by;
Still one by one, in swift succession, pass
The gliding shadows o'er the polish'd glass.
This lady's charms the nicest could not blame,
But vile suspicions had aspersed her fame;
That was with sense, but not with virtue blest:
And one had grace; that wanted all the rest.
Thus doubting long what nymph should be his prize,
He fix'd at last upon ELIZA's eyes.
Her faults he knew not; love is always blind;
But every charm revolved within his mind:
Her tender age, her form divinely fair;
Her easy motion, her attractive air;
Her sweet behavior, her enchanting face;
Her moving softness, and majestic grace.
Much in his prudence did Old WARD rejoice,
And thought no mortal could dispute his choice:

Once more in haste he summon'd every friend,
And told them all their pains were at an end,
Heaven that (said he) inspired me first to wed,
Provides a second consort for my bed ;
Let none oppose th' election, since on this
Depends my present, and my future bliss.

A dame there is, the darling of my eyes,
Young, beauteous, artless, innocent and wise ; Chaste,
tho' not rich ; and tho' not highly born,
Of honest parents, and may serve my turn.
Her will I love, if gracious Heaven so please,
And pass my age in sanctity and ease.

This BOWEN heard, nor could his spleen control,
Touch'd to the quick and soured at the soul.
Dear Sir, he cried, if this be all you dread,
Heaven put it past a doubt that you are wed;
And to my fervent prayers so far consent,
That ere your love begins you may repent.
Good Heaven, no doubt, your gushing state approves,
Since it chastises still what best it loves.

Yet be not, Sir, abandon'd to despair ;
Seek, and you'll find one more among the fair,
One that may do your business to a hair ;
Not e'en in wish your happiness delay,
But prove the scourge to lash you on your way;
Then to the skies your mounting soul shall go,
Swift as an arrow soaring from the bow !

Provided still you moderate your joy,
Nor in your pleasures all your strength employ.
Let reason's rule your strong desires abate,
Nor please too lavishly your gentle mate.
Old wives there are, of judgment most acute,
Who solve these questions beyond all dispute;
Consult with those, and be of better cheer;
Be gay, do penance, and dismiss your fear.
So said, they rose, nor more the work delay'd;
The snare was fix'd and the proposal made.
Nor was it hard to move the lady's mind;
When fortune favors, still the fair are kind.
WARD's true inwardness was overcharged with bliss
In sealing love with a paroxysmal kiss.

I'll pass their cooing, and each minor deed,
Too long for me to write, or you to read,
Nor will, with quaint impertinence, display
Our Pastor's strut, or Plymouth's proud array.
The time approach'd; to bed the parties went,
At once with carnal and devout intent.
Old BEECHER pray'd, and bade the moral wife
Like SARAH or REBECCA lead her life;
Then ask'd the powers the red lounge to bless,
And made all sure enough with holiness.
And now the Plymouth gates are opened wide,
The guests appear in order, side by side,
The breathing flute's soft notes are heard around,
And the shrill trumpets mix their silver sound;

The vaulted roofs with echoing music ring;
These touch the vocal stops, and those the trembling
    string.
Not thus AMPHION turned the warbling lyre,
Nor JOAB the sounding clarion could inspire,
Nor fierce THEODAMAS, whose sprightly strain
Could swell the soul to rage, and fire the martial train.

    BACCHUS himself, the nuptial feast to grace,
(So poets sing) was present on the place:
And lovely VENUS, goddess of delight,
With parting lips, exquisite, warm and bright,
Shook high her flaming torch in open view,
And danced around, and smiled on all the crew;
Pleased her best servant would his courage try,
No less in wedlock than in liberty.
Full many an age sweet CUPID had not spied
So gross a bridegroom with so small a bride.
Ye bards! renown'd among the tuneful throng
For gentle lays, and joyous nuptial song,
Think not your softest numbers can display
The matchless glories of this blissful day;
The joys are such, as far transcend your rage,
When tender youth feels so-so to old age.

    The beauteous dame sat smiling at the board,
And darted amorous glances at Old WARD.
Not ESTHER's self, whose charms the Hebrews sing,
E'er look'd so lovely on her Persian king;

Bright as the rising sun in summer's day,
And fresh and blooming as the mouth of May!
The joyful WARD surveyed her by his side,
Nor envied PARIS with the Spartan bride;
Still as his mind revolved with vast delight,
The entrancing raptures of the approaching night,
Restless he sate, invoking every power,
To speed his bliss, and haste the happy hour.
Meantime the vigorous dancers beat the ground,
And songs were sung, and flowing bowls went round.
With odorous flowers they perfum'd the place,
And mirth and pleasure shone in every face.
WILLIAM alone, of all the menial train,
Sad in the midst of triumphs, sigh'd for pain;
WILLIAM alone, the husband and the sire,
Consum'd at heart, and fed a secret fire.
His lovely mistress all his soul possess'd,
He look'd, he languish'd, and could take no rest.
His task perform'd, he sadly went his way,
Fell on his bed, and loathed the light of day.
There let him lie, till his relenting dame
Weep in her turn, and waste in equal flame.

The weary sun, as learned poets write,
Forsook the horizon, and roll'd down the light ;
While glittering stars his absent beams supply
And night's dark mantle overspread the sky.
Then rose the guests, and, as the time required,
Each paid his thanks, and decently retired.

The foe once gone, Old WARD prepared to undress,
So keen he was, and eager to possess.
Upon his knee he drew the pliant dame,
Then read from " Norwood " lines that spake his flame.
" ELIZA dear, how do you feel ? " (he sighed).
" So-so, dear Father," (the buxom dame replied).

Full soon the sheets were spread and BESS undress'd;
The room was perfum'd, the red lounge was bless'd.
What next ensued beseems not me to say ;
'Tis sung he labored till the dawning day;
Then briskly sprung from bed with heart so light,
As all were nothing he had done by night;
And sipped his cordial as he sat upright.
He kissed his balmy BESS with wanton play,
And feebly sung a lusty roundelay:
Then on the lounge his weary limbs he cast;
For every labor must have rest at last.
But anxious cares his noble soul oppress'd;
Sleep fled his eyes, and peace forsook his breast.
The raging flames that in his bosom dwell,
He wanted art to hide, and means to tell.
But, opening wide his expansive vest,
He wrote a song that sweet ELIZA blest;
Which, writ and folded with the nicest art,
He wrapp'd in silk, and laid it on his heart.

When now, the fourth revolving day was run,
('Twas June, and Cancer had received the sun),

Forth from the red lounge came the beautious bride;
Her lusty WARD moved slowly by her side.
High notes he sung; they feasted in the hall;
The servants round stood ready at their call.

WILLIAM alone was absent from the board,
And much his sickness grieved the loving WARD,
Who pray'd ELIZA, attended with her train,
To visit WILLIAM and divert his pain.
The obliging dames obey'd with one consent;
They left the hall and to his lodging went.
The female tribe surround him in undress,
And close beside him sat the gentle BESS;
Where, as she tried his pulse, he softly drew
A heaving sigh, and cast a mournful view.
Then gave his bill, and bribed the powers divine,
With secret vows, to favor his design.

Who studies now but discontented BESS?
On her red lounge she feels her love's distress.
The lumpish BEECHER snored away the night,
Till snorts awaked him near the morning light.
What then he did I'll not presume to tell,
Nor if she thought herself in heaven or hell.
Honest and dull upon the lounge they lay
Till the bell toll'd, and then arose to pray.

Were it by forceful destiny decreed,
Or did from chance or Nature's power proceed,

Or that same star, with aspect kind to love,
Shed its selectest influence from above;
Whatever was the cause, the tender dame
Felt the first motions of an infant flame.
Ye fair, draw near; let her example move
Your gentle minds to pity those who love!
Had some fierce tyrant in her stead been found,
The poor adorer sure had hang'd or drown'd;
But she, your sex's mirror, free from pride,
Was much too meek to prove a homicide.

   But to my tale: Some sages have defined
Pleasure the sovereign bliss of human kind.
BEECHER, who studied much, we may suppose,
Derived his high philosophy from those,
For, like a prince, he bore the vast expense
Of blooded steeds and proud magnificence;
His house was stately, his retinue gay,
Large was his train, and gorgeous his array.
His spacious garden, made to yield to none,
Was compass'd round with walls of solid stone ;
PRIAPUS could not half describe the grace
(Though God of Gardens) of this charming place ;
A place to tire the rambling wits of France
In long descriptions, and exceed romance ;
Enough to shame the gentlest bard that sings
Of painted meadows, and of purling springs.

   Full in the centre of the flowery ground
A crystal fountain spread its streams around,

The fruitful banks with verdant laurels crown'd ;
About this spring (if what we hear is true)
The dapper elves their moonlight sports pursue ;
Their pigmy king, and little fairy queen,
In circling dances gambol'd on the green,
While tuneful sprites a merry concert made,
And airy music warbled through the shade.

Hither BEECHER in silence would repair,
(His scene of pleasure and peculiar care) ;
For this he held it dear, and always bore
The silver key that lock'd the garden door.
To this sweet place, in Summer's sultry heat,
He used, from noise and business, to retreat,
And here in dalliance spend the livelong day,
With dear ELIZA, charming, sweet and gay.
But ah, what mortal lives of bliss secure ?
How short a space our worldly joys endure !
O Fortune, fair, like all thy treach'rous kind,
But faithless still, and wav'ring as the wind !
O painted monster, form'd mankind to cheat
With pleasing poison, and with soft deceit !
This old, this amorous, this gushing prig,
Amidst his ease, his solace, and his swig,
Struck dumb by thee, resigns his days to grief,
And calls on death, the wretch's last relief.

The rage of jealousy then seized his mind,
For much he feared the faith of womankind.

Poor Bess, not suffered from his side to go,
Was captive kept : he watched and loved her so :
And should he chance in revel spend a night,
He pulled her bell before the morning light.
Should she abroad for health or pleasure stray,
" Write me, love," he cries, "for my wife's away.
On you I pray God's blessing for to rest ;
Till you return, there's none to warm my nest.
Your latest note, like Spring on Winter, broke,
And gave an inward rebound to love's yoke.
No one can ever know, none but my God,
Through what a dreary wilderness I've trod ;
There was Mount Sinai and the barren sand ;
Sad pilgrimage was marked on every hand ;
There was reversal 'twixt despair and hope,
Through which the weary had to live and grope.
Shall I, like Moses, on the border die,
Or wait the Promised Land, and for you sigh?
As round your nest to forage I delight,
You are my star, whose rays are warm and bright.

Bess looked on William with a lover's eye ;
For, oh, 'twas fix'd ; she must possess or die !
Nor less impatience vexed her amorous Will,
Wild with delay, and smoking like a kiln.
Watched as she was, yet could he not refrain
By secret writing to disclose his pain :
The dame by signs revealed her kind intent,
Till both were conscious what each other meant.

Ah, simple WARD, what would thy eyes avail
Though they could see as far as ships can sail?
ARGUS himself, so cautious and so wise,
Was overmatched, for all his hundred eyes:
So many an honest husband may, 'tis known,
Who, wisely, never thinks the case his own.

The dame, at last, by diligence and care,
Procured the key which WARD was wont to bear;
She took the wards in wax before the fire,
And gave the impression to the trusty squire.
By means of this some wonder shall appear,
Which, in due place and season, you may hear.

Well sung sweet OVID, in the days of yore,
What slight is that which love will not explore?
And PYRAMUS and THISBE plainly show
The feats true lovers, when they list, can do:
Though watched and captive, yet, in spite of all,
They found the art of kissing through a wall.

But now no longer from our tale to stray,
It happened once, upon a Summer's day,
Our reverend Priest was urged to amorous play:
He raised his BESS, ere matin-bell was rung,
And thus his morning canticle he sung:

"Awake, my love, disclose thy radiant eyes:
Arise, my BESS, my beauteous lady, rise!

Hear how the doves with pensive notes complain,
And in soft murmurs tell the trees their pain.
The Winter's past; the clouds and tempests fly;
The sun adorns the fields, and brightens all the sky.
Fair without spot, whose every charming part
My bosom wounds and captivates my heart,
Come, and in mutual pleasures let's engage,
Joy of my life, and comfort of my age."
This heard, to WILLIAM straight a sign she made
To haste before; the gentle WILL obeyed;
Secret and undescried he took his way,
And, ambush'd close, behind an arbor lay.

It was not long ere puffing BEECHER came,
And hand in hand with him his lovely dame;
Dumb as he was, not doubting all was sure,
He turned the key, and made the gate secure.

" Here let us walk," he said, " observed by none,
Conscious of pleasures to the world unknown:
So may my soul have joy, as thou, fond wife,
Art far the dearest solace of my life:
And rather would I choose, by Heaven above,
To die this instant, than to lose thy love.
Reflect what truth was in my passion shown,
When, dumpy dear, I took thee for my own,
And sought no beauty but thine alone.
Old as I am, my vigor still is sound;
I'll prove your match in hugging, I'll be bound,

Nor age nor labor weigh my antics down.
Each other loss with patience I can bear,
The loss of thee is what I only fear.

Consider then, my BESSIE and my wife,
Our solid comforts midst this wordly strife.
At first the love of CHRIST himself you gain;
Next, your own honor undefil'd maintain;
And, lastly, that which sure your mind must move,
My heart and soul shall gratify your love.
Make your own terms, and ere to-morrow's sun
Displays his light, by Heaven it shall be done.
I seal the contract with a holy kiss,
And will perform, by this—my dear, and this ;
Have comfort, BESS, nor think thy WARD unkind ;
'Tis love, not jealousy, that fires my mind ;
For when thy charms my sober thoughts engage,
And joined to them my own unequal age,
From thy dear side I have no power to part,
Such secret transports warm my melting heart.
For who that once possess'd those heavenly charms,
Could live one moment absent from thy arms ? "

He ceased, and BESS with modest grace replied—
(Weak was her voice, as while she spoke she cried) :
" Heaven knows (with that a tender sigh she drew)
I have a soul to save as well as you;
And, what no less you to my charge commend,
My dearest honor, will to death defend.

To you, on the red lounge, I gave my hand,
And joined my heart in Cupid's sacred band;
Yet, after this, if you distrust my care,
Then, BEECHER, hear, and witness what I swear:

First may the yawning earth her bosom rend,
And let me hence to hell alive descend;
Or die the death I dread no less than hell,
Sewed in a sack, and plunged into a well:
Ere I my fame by one lewd act disgrace,
Or once renounce the honor of my race.
For, BEECHER, know, of gentle blood I came ;
I loathe a punk, and startle at the name.
But jealous men on their own crimes reflect,
And learn from thence their ladies to suspect ;
Else why these needless cautions, WARD, to me ?
Those doubts and fears of female constancy !
This chime still rings in every lady's ear,
The only strain your love must hope to hear."

Thus, while she spoke, a sidelong glance she cast
Where WILLIAM, kneeling, worship'd as she past.
She saw him watch the motion of her eye,
And singled out a pear-tree planted nigh :
'Twas charged with fruit, which made a goodly
show, And hung with dangling pears was every
bough. Thither obsequious WILLIAM addressed his
pace,
And climbing, in the summit took his place ;

WARD and ELIZA walked beneath in view,
Where let us leave them, and our tale pursue.

'Twas now the season when the glorious sun
His heavenly progress through the Twins had run ;
And JOVE, exalted, his mild influence yields
To glad the glebe, and paint the flowery fields ;
Clear was the day, and PHŒBUS, rising bright,
Had streaked the azure firmament with light ;
He pierced the glittering clouds with golden streams,
And warmed the womb of earth with genial beams.

It so befell, in that fair morning-tide,
The gossips sported on the garden side,
And in the midst FRANK MOULTON and his bride.
So featly tripp'd the light-foot ladies 'round,
The men so nimbly o'er the green sward bound,
That scarce they bent the flowers or touch'd the ground.
The dances ended, all the merry train
For pinks and daisies searched the flowery plain ;
While on the bank reclined of rising green,
Thus, with a frown, the king bespoke his queen :

'Tis too apparent, argue what you can,
The treachery you women use to man ;
A thousand authors have this truth made out,
And sad experience leaves no room for doubt.

Heaven rest thy spirit, noble SOLOMON,
A wiser monarch never saw the sun :

All wealth, all honors, the supreme degree
Of earthly bliss, was well bestow'd on thee!
For sagely hast thou said : Of all mankind,
One only just and righteous hope to find:
But shouldst thou search the spacious world around,
Yet one good woman is not to be found.

Thus says the king who knew your wickedness ;
The son of SIRACH testifies no less.
So may some wild-fire on your bodies fall,
Or some devouring flame consume you all,
As well you view the lecher in the tree,
And well this venerable man you see :
But since he's dumb and old (a helpless case),
His groom shall cuckold him before your face.

Now, by my own dread majesty I swear,
And by this awful sceptre that I bear,
No impious wretch shall 'scape unpunished long
That in my presence offers such a wrong.
I will this instant undeceive him quite,
And, in the very act, show him the sight :
And set the doxy here in open view,
A warning to these ladies and to you,
And all the faithless sex, forever to be true."

"And will you so," replied the queen, "indeed!
Now, by my mother's soul, it is decreed,
She shall not want an answer at her need.

For her, and for her daughters, I'll engage,
And all the sex in each succeeding age ;
Art shall be theirs to varnish an offence,
And fortify their crimes with confidence.
Nay, were they taken in a strict embrace,
Seen with both eyes, and pinion'd on the place ;
All they shall need is to protest and swear,
Breathe a soft sigh, and drop a tender tear ;
Till their wise husbands, gull'd by arts like these,
Grow gentle, tractable, and tame as geese.

What though this slanderous Jew, this SOLOMON,
Call'd women fools, and knew full many a one ?
The wiser wits of later times declare
How constant, chaste, and virtuous, women are.
Witness the martyrs, who resigned their breath,
Serene in torments, unconcerned in death ;
And witness next what Roman authors tell,
How ARRIA, PORTIA, and LUCRETIA fell.

But since the sacred leaves to all are free,
And men interpret texts, why should not we ?
By this no more was meant than to have shown
That sovereign goodness dwells in him alone
Who only Is, and is but only One.
But grant the worst ; shall women then be weigh'd
By every word that SOLOMON has said ?
What though this king (as ancient story boasts)
Built a fair temple to the Lord of Hosts ;

He ceased, at last, his Maker to adore,
And did as much for idol gods, or more.
Beware what lavish praises you confer
On a rank lecher and idolator,
Whose reign indulgent Go**, says Holy Writ,
Did but for DAVID's righteous sake permit ;
DAVID, the monarch after Heaven's own hand,
Who loved our sex, and honored all our kind.

Well, I'm a woman, and as such must speak ;
Silence would swell me, and my heart would break.
Know, then, I scorn your dull authorities,
Your idle wits, and all their learned lies.
By Heaven, those authors are our sex's foes,
Whom, in our right, I must and will oppose.

Nay, (quoth the king,) dear madam, be not wroth ;
I yield it up ; but since I gave my oath
That this much injured Priest the sight must see,
It must be done ;—I am a king, (said he),
And one whose faith has ever sacred been.

And so has mine, (she said)—I am a queen :
Her answer she shall have, I undertake ;
And thus an end of all dispute I make.
Try when you list, and you shall find, my lord,
It is not in our sex to break our word.

We leave them here in this heroic strain,
And to Old WARD our story turns again;

Who in the garden, with his lovely BESS,
Sits on the ragged edge of sad distress.

Now, sighing as he went, at last he drew,
By easy steps, to where the pear-tree grew:
The longing dame look'd up, and spied her love
Full fairly perch'd among the boughs above.
She stopp'd, and sighing—oh! good gods, she cried,
What pangs, what sudden shoots, distend my side!
O for that tempting fruit, so fresh, so green!
Help, for the love of Heaven's immortal queen;
Help, dearest WARD, and save at once the life
Of thy poor infant, and thy longing wife!

Sore sigh'd Old WARD to hear his BESSIE cry,
But could not climb, and had no servant nigh:
Old as he was, and big and flaccid too,
What could, alas! the helpless BEECHER do?

And must I languish, then, (she said,) and die,
Yet view the lovely fruit before my eye?
At least, dear WARD, for Charity's sweet sake,
Vouchsafe the trunk between your arms to take;
Then from your back I might ascend the tree:
Do you but stoop, and leave the rest to me.

With all my soul, he thus replied, again;
I'd spend my dearest blood to ease thy pain.

With that his back against the trunk he bent;
She seized a twig, and up the tree she went.

Now, prove your patience, gentle ladies all,
Nor let on me your heavy anger fall :
'Tis truth I tell, though not in phrase refin'd;
Though blunt my tale, yet honest is my mind.
What feats the lady in the tree might do
I pass, as gambols never known to you;
But sure it was a merrier fit, she swore,
Than in her life she ever felt before.
In that nice moment BEECHER had a fright,
And, looking up, he saw a wondrous sight.
Straight on the tree his eager eyes he bent,
As one whose thoughts were on his spouse intent;
But when he saw his bosom BESS so dress'd,
His rage was such as cannot be express'd ;
Not frantic mothers, when their infants die,
With louder clamors rend the vaulted sky :
He cried, he roared, he stormed, he tore his hair ;
" Death ! hell ! and furies ! what dost thou do there ? "

" What ails my dear ? " the trembling BESS replied ;
" I thought your patience had been better tried :
Is it for this, ungrateful and unkind,
To save your strength, a friend in need I find ?
Why was I taught to prove that love was free
By struggling with a man upon a tree ? "

"If this be struggling, by the Holy Word,
'Tis struggling with a vengeance," quoth Old WARD.

" Guard me, good angels," cried the gentle BESS;
"I fear my darling is in much distress.
Alas! my love! if you could rightly see,
You ne'er had used those bitter words to me;
So help me, fates, as 'tis no perfect sight,
But some faint glimmering of a doubtful light."

" What I have said (quoth he) I must maintain,
For by the immortal pow'rs, it *seemed* too plain."

" By all those powers, some frenzy seized your mind,
(Replied the dame); are these the thanks I find?
Wretch that I am that e'er I was so kind!"
She said; a rising sigh expressed her woe;
The ready tears apace began to flow,
And as they fell, she wiped from either eye
The drops (for women, when they list, can cry).

BEECHER was touch'd; and in his looks appeared
Signs of remorse, while thus his spouse he cheered:

" BESSIE, 'tis past, and my short anger o'er!
Kiss me, and vex your tender heart no more;
Excuse me, dear, if aught amiss was said,
For, by my Church, amends shall soon be made:

Let my repentance your forgiveness draw;
By Heaven, I swore but what I *thought* I saw."

"Ah, my loved WARD! 'twas much unkind (she cried)
On bare suspicion thus to be belied.
For months you have of hazy sight complained;
You're e'er in doubt until the sight's regained.
But till it is establish'd, for a while
Imperfect objects may your sense beguile.
Thus when from sleep we first our eyes display,
The balls are wounded with the piercing ray,
And dusky vapors rise and intercept the day:
Then, dear, be cautious, nor too rashly deem;
Heaven knows how seldom things are what they seem!
Consult your reason, and you soon shall find
'Twas you were jealous, not your BESS unkind:
JOVE ne'er spoke oracle more true than this:
None judge so wrong as those who think amiss."

With that she leap'd into Old WARD's embrace,
With well-dissembled virtue in her face.
He hugg'd her close, and kiss'd her o'er and o'er,
Disturb'd with doubts and jealousies no more:
Both, pleased and bless'd, renew'd their mutual kiss,
Both full of joy, true inwardness, and bliss.

Thus ends our tale, whose moral next to make:
Let all wise husbands hence example take;
And pray, to crown the pleasure of their lives,
To be so well deluded by their wives.

For troubles sore, WARD had his pension raised;
For which let BEACH and Plymouth Church be praised.

  While all must smile, e'en those grown cross with
     gout,
We take our hat, and now step down and out.

 END.

Milton Keynes UK
Ingram Content Group UK Ltd.
UKHW020902290324
440175UK00004B/520